MW01144072

TI AND THE MAGICAL KEY

Where the sky is born

ISBN-13: 978-1519726773

Xaman Ek

Balam

Quetzal

Mangrove

Coati

Manatee

Lak'in

Kiik Tukuul

PRONUNCIATION GUIDE

Ti: _____tee
Nuuk Ha: _____nook-há
Atan: _____ah-tún
Laak´: _____luck
Tat: _____tat
Itzamna: _____eet-sum-ná
Ixchel: _____eek-shéll
Kukulkan: _____koo-cool-kán
Chac: _____chuck
Xaman Ek: _____shah-man-éck
Ixcacao: _____eesh-ka-ców
Chichen Itza: _____chee-che-neetzá
Tulum: _____too-loóm
Sian Ka´an: _____see-an-kán
Muyil: _____moo-yéel
Cozumel: _____kah-zoo-mél
Ceiba: _____say-báh
Kiik: _____keek
Tukuul: _____too-coól
Lak´in: _____la-kéen
Balam: _____ba-lám
Quetzal: _____kwet-zál
Coati: _____kwa-tée

We would like to acknowledge the team
that made this creation possible.
Our daughter and inspiration Nelie, we love you!
Our families who have always been there
no matter what direction we took.
Sylvia, Mike, Charlotte, Sandy, Rick, Karen, Iri,
Moksha, Vanessa and Tamara, thank you!

Editor: Cara Bianca Patik

ITZAMNA'S SPELL

"Only a human with a pure heart has the power to unite the keys and give them back their magic."

PROLOGUE

Many moons ago, Itzamna, one of the most powerful gods of the Mayans, announced the return of the god of the wind, Kukulkan. Itzamna suspected that Kukulkan was not up to any good, and as a precaution the deity decided to hide THE KEY he had created to protect everyone's happiness.

To diffuse the power of the magical object, Itzamna secretly punched smaller keys out of the original one and handed them over to the Shaman Tat. Tat hid the small keys at different locations far away from where he lived in Chichen Itza, hoping Kukulkan wouldn't be able to find them. The frame of THE KEY stayed with Itzamna.

Years later with the aid of Itzamna's wife, Ixchel, Kukulkan stole the frame and is now looking for the hidden keys so he can become the most powerful of all the gods.

Itzamna was suspicious that Kukulkan wanted to possess the smaller keys, so he carefully selected Ti, a young boy with a pure heart, to go on the journey to find the keys before Kukulkan could.

And thus began the story and the race for the magical keys.

1

Cautious footsteps were the first indication that someone had crossed the entrance to the hiding place. The smell of humidity and dust hung in the air. It was only the second time anyone had entered since the frame of THE KEY, the symbol of happiness, had been stored here for its safety. The invader advanced quickly, heavy breaths accompanying the sound of his steps. A hand reached forward and nervously started searching for something, but only groped thin air.

"It's gone! He really stole the frame of THE KEY," Itzamna exclaimed.

The deity clenched his fist angrily. "Kukulkan, I want you to listen carefully. I will make sure you won't get the small keys. You will have to fight me over this. Do you hear me?!" Infuriated, Itzamna headed towards the exit.

"I have to check on the boy and his parents. Hopefully they have already found one of the keys." And with these words, total silence returned to the place that had failed to protect the frame.

2

Branches ripped off trees with a loud crack and blew like leaves through the air. Even the strong trunks bent down to the ground, obeying the power of the wind. Stones began rolling as if attempting to escape the storm.

"What's happening?" Ti shouted, his voice trying to cut through the noise of the wind.

"We need to look for shelter. Come on, we have to hurry!" Nuuk Ha bellowed back.

At exactly that moment an enormous lightning bolt struck through the clouds, hitting the ground as if it wanted to destroy it. Ti looked up to the sky and froze. At first he couldn't tell what was emerging from the sky, seemingly coming straight towards him. The closer it got, the more it started to look like a serpent with feathers.

"So it's you Itzamna sent to find the keys. Give me the key you silly boy. Give it to me!!!!!" the serpent roared.

Ti stumbled backwards, staring in disbelief at what he was seeing. "Who are you?"

"Who am I?! I am Kukulkan, the god of the wind. Fear me!" the god exploded angrily and changed his face into its human form.

"Why are you doing this?" Ti shouted, pointing at the destruction the storm was causing.

"You have something that belongs to me. Give me the key you found in the temple and tell me where the other keys are hidden," Kukulkan demanded.

"I don't know where the other keys are," Ti replied truthfully.

"You are a liar!" The god howled indignantly and disappeared back into the clouds.

"RUN!" Nuuk Ha shouted. Ti looked at the turtle and saw her eyes filled with fear. "Look!" she exclaimed, pointing towards the ocean. The waves appeared to be uniting themselves. The water rose, higher and higher until it erupted through the dark sky, aiming for land. Ti grabbed the turtle and started running faster than he had ever thought possible, trying to reach the jungle before the waves came crashing onto land.

Deeper and deeper into the green thicket they ran. Branches cut into his face, but he didn't feel the pain. All Ti could think of was a safe place to hide. He ran and ran until his feet suddenly lost ground. Ti couldn't tell for how long they fell, but it felt like a lifetime. Holding one of Nuuk Ha's feet tightly in his hand, the darkness closed in around them.

When his feet touched the cool water Ti closed his eyes and allowed himself to be immersed, keeping hold of Nuuk Ha all the while. They floated weightlessly in the darkness until he opened his eyes and a beam of sunlight finally guided him up to the surface of the water.

3

Itzamna sat bent over a calendar when Xaman Ek, the god of travelers, entered the room.

Itzamna looked up. "Did you find the boy and his parents who I sent to find the keys?" he asked.

"Yes, I found them. But so did Kukulkan. He knows the boy has the first key," the god of travelers informed Itzamna with concern.

Itzamna froze in light of the news. "Impossible. Nobody knew that I sent the boy on the journey."

"I'm afraid that Kukulkan just tried to attack him. We have witnesses."

"Where is the boy right now?" Itzamna asked, worried.

"I lost him when he fell into a sinkhole. The communication with the underworld is always so difficult!" Xaman Ek explained, shaking his head.

"We have to find the boy before Kukulkan gets him," replied Itzamna urgently and walked hastily out of the room.

"Where are we?" Ti asked, floating on his back and squinting. Sunshine was falling through the opening of the roof, gently tickling his face.

"I don't know, but this is definitely fresh water and not seawater," the turtle replied after taking a sip and spitting it out in disgust.

"See the roots of the tree coming down all the way from above? It feels like we are below the earth," Ti said in wonder.

Nuuk Ha looked around. "It looks like we are in a sinkhole," she concluded.

"A sinkhole? We shouldn't be here. We have to get out as fast as we can!" Ti shouted.

"Why the rush?" the turtle asked, alarmed.

"We have entered the underworld. The Lords of Death live here!"

"But how do we get back up?" Nuuk Ha asked, staring at the hole of the cave high above them.

"I don't think we can. But it seems as though the cave continues over there," Ti replied, pointing at the opposite side. "Maybe there's a river of some sort."

"It's really dark over there," Nuuk Ha stammered in fear.

"Well, we either face the darkness
or stay here forever," Ti reasoned.
"Ok, ok, but let's swim slowly
so we don't lose each other,"
and the turtle and Ti began
swimming towards the
dark hole.

5

"Did you find him? Did you get the key?" Ixchel asked excitedly.

"No, I lost the boy in the jungle. But the key is as good as mine. He is just a boy," Kukulkan replied confidently.

"But your powers are not as strong in the jungle as they are in the ocean," Ixchel pointed out. "Perhaps it's time to call him."

"You might be right," Kukulkan replied, considering for a moment. "Yes, let me call him." The god turned around and released a chirping sound to all four cardinal points. The colors of the sky began to change. The east turned a flaming red, the north a brilliant white, the west the darkest of blacks, and the south a fierce yellow. Excitement seized the god as he watched his powers materialize.

"He will be here soon," Kukulkan pronounced.

6

Total darkness and silence embraced the two swimmers once they entered the tunnel. Neither one said a word. The underground river became increasingly narrow and the smell of wet stone became stronger the further they got. The cave's ceiling began to slope down, almost touching the surface of the water. Soon it was so low they had to dive underwater, hoping they would find a spot to breathe a little further along. Here and there a ray of sunlight fell through the ceiling revealing the beauty of the mystical underwater world.

When they finally reached a spot where the cave expanded, Ti suggested a rest. Huge stalactites hung from the limestone ceiling as if trying to greet their opposites on the ground. The cave looked both majestic and intimidating.

Sitting down, Ti confessed: "When we were at the ocean I was really scared."

"And you should have been," Nuuk Ha responded. "I have seen a lot of my friends get hurt during Kukulkan's attacks."

"So that was not the first time it happened?" Ti asked, astounded.

"Oh no! This has been going on for...." The turtle paused to concentrate. "I would say years. Although I am certain it never happened before your grandfather Tat came to hide the keys."

"Are you suggesting it has something to do with Tat?" asked Ti.

"I'm not sure, but Kukulkan was very angry, and I heard him scream 'Give me the key'. This key of yours seems to be really important to him."

"True. He did want the key," Ti said absently while pulling the tiny key out of his shell to look at it. "Nuuk Ha," Ti whispered. "I hope my parents are safe. I'm worried about them."

"Don't be!" the turtle replied encouragingly. "I saw them with a friend of mine running into the jungle. I'm sure they are safe. We'll find them."

Ti's father stood with his back to the fire he had lit, glaring into the darkness of the jungle. The small raccoon-like coati that had helped him and his wife escape the hurricane in Tulum was snoring comfortably in the lap of Ti's mother, Atan.

"Laak, I hope Ti is ok," Atan sobbed softly while petting the friendly animal.

Ti's father turned around and slowly kneeled down to put his arms around her. "Don't cry. We raised him. You have to trust that we gave him everything he needs to survive," Laak' answered reassuringly, staring into the fire.

"But tomorrow we will start looking for him."

8

While still resting in the cave, Nuuk Ha spoke: "let's try to solve the riddle your grandfather gave us," she proposed. "Let's see: 'where the sky is born. *Where the land is torn. Where the pie misses corn. Where the fly has a horn'.*"

"It doesn't make any sense!" Ti said, discouraged.

"I was just thinking out loud," Nuuk Ha replied defensively.

"What are *you* doing here?!" a loud voice suddenly echoed through the cave.

"Uhm, that wasn't you talking, right?!" Nuuk Ha asked frightened, looking at Ti.

"No, it was me!" A large shadow holding an axe suddenly appeared.

"Oh boy," the turtle exclaimed. After clearing her throat, she continued: "nice to meet you. This is my friend Ti and I am Nuuk Ha. You have a beautiful place here. What's your name?"

"I am Chac, the god of rain, and this is the underworld. Not a happy place, may I add."

The lump in Nuuk Ha's throat seemed to get bigger and bigger.

"Say something," the turtle whispered to Ti.

"That's a beautiful axe," Ti attempted.

The turtle stared at Ti in disbelief. "Don't mention the axe!" she whispered urgently.

Turning back to the god of rain, Nuuk Ha continued: "well, dear Chac, we did not come to disturb you and are ready to leave your beloved home right now. So goodbye!" said the turtle, crawling towards the water.

"Hold it!" Chac shouted. "Nobody just leaves the underworld. You must give me a gift before making your departure."

Instinctively, Ti reached for the key he had shoved back in his golden shell. He looked at his friend and silently formed the words, "Not the key."

Nuuk Ha nodded. "The problem is we have nothing to give you," she said apologetically.

"That is not good. NOT good. In that case, one of *you* has to be my gift," the god replied.

"Unfortunately, we are on a very important journey, so I'm afraid that won't be possible," Nuuk Ha explained, feeling the lump in her throat growing again. "We just escaped a hurricane and have to find our way to *'where the sky is born'*."

"A hurricane? Who commanded it?" Chac demanded furiously.

"Kukulkan did," Ti said, finally finding his voice.

"Kukulkan??!!! *I* want to do the hurricanes. Me, me, *me!*" The deity started swinging his axe in anger.

"Is there something we can do to help?" Ti asked.

"Not from down here," the god replied, annoyed. After a moment of reflection, Chac decided. "Ok, you may continue your journey to Sian Ka'an, but you have to find a way to stop Kukulkan from creating the hurricanes. I will then generously forget about taking one of you as a gift. But next time I see you in a sinkhole, I will call the Lords of Death and one of you stays. Understood?"

"Wonderful idea!" Nuuk Ha said, pulling Ti along with her towards the water.

When Chac was out of sight and Ti felt far enough away from the axe-swinging god, he yelled back: "what is Sian Ka'an?"

"*'The place where the sky is born'.* Just keep following the river and you will get there. Now leave me alone or I will change my mind and one of you will stay," Chac shouted in return.

"Keep swimming!" Nuuk Ha urged, and the darkness welcomed them back into its fold.

"I see him!" Ixchel shouted excitedly.

A small red fireball appeared far above in the sky. The closer it got, the more obvious it became that it was a beautiful bird whose rich red belly sprouted sparkling long feathers of blue and green.

"Greetings Quetzal," Kukulkan welcomed the bird, stretching out his arm for him to land on. Softly the bird rested his talons on the offered forearm, bowed and watched the deity attentively.

"I need your help my friend. You have to find someone. It is a boy who has something that's mine. Can you do that for me?" Kukulkan asked.

The bird chirped in agreement, and took off to find Ti.

"Light! Lots of light!" Nuuk Ha happily shouted.

A huge opening appeared ahead. The river emerged into open air and allowed them to finally climb out of the cave. Beautiful white water lilies surrounded the opening and captivated them with their sweet scent.

"We're still in the jungle. How do we find Sian Ka'an?" Ti wondered.

"I'd say we follow the river as Chac suggested. It *has* to come out at the ocean at some point. I have lots of friends at the sea. Someone will know the way to Sian Ka'an in case we get lost," the turtle proposed.

"Ok, let's get moving," the boy said and lifted up Nuuk Ha to travel on his back.

After a day, they finally reached the ocean. Nuuk Ha excitedly pointed towards the water.

"What?" Ti asked, not understanding what the turtle wanted to show him.

"Don't you see our friends? They're right in front of us!"

"With all due respect, there's no one there," Ti said.

"I'm not talking about people! I'm talking about plants!"

"Plants?" Ti wondered, when he saw a pair of huge friendly eyes peering out at him.

"Helloooooo!" it bellowed.

The leafy tree seemed to wave at them with its bony, woody arms.

Ti stepped back. "Woah, what is that? I mean, *who* is that?"

"They are Mangroves. Let's go talk to them," said the turtle.

"Oh so pleased to meet you'sss," the tree said, waving her head in excitement and blinking her eyes a little too quickly.

"Same here!" Ti said, still not convinced as to why he was talking to a tree.

"Oops, are your feet getting wet'sss?" the mangrove asked. "Sorry dear, but I like it muddy'sss."

"The poor thing has an articulation problem," Ti whispered behind his hand to the turtle.

"No, that's not the tree hissing. It's the snake in her crown," Nuuk Ha explained amused. "Snakes like to relax there. And you will also find lots of shells and barnacles living on her branches," she continued.

"So the mangrove gives a home to a lot of different animals," Ti summarized.

"Yes, we like having company. More Fun'sss," said the tree, blinking her big eyes.

"I still don't understand why you said she is our friend," Ti pointed out.

"Because they are protecting our beaches," the turtle replied.

"Oh wow! The tree does?" Ti said with a curious look at the mangrove. "But it smells a little," the boy added, waving his hand in front of his nose.

Nuuk Ha giggled. "Yes, she does not smell the best. It's because mangroves filter the water so that it stays clean."

"She deserves to look a lot prettier for all she does. I would have never paid attention to it. It's so... tree-y," faltered Ti.

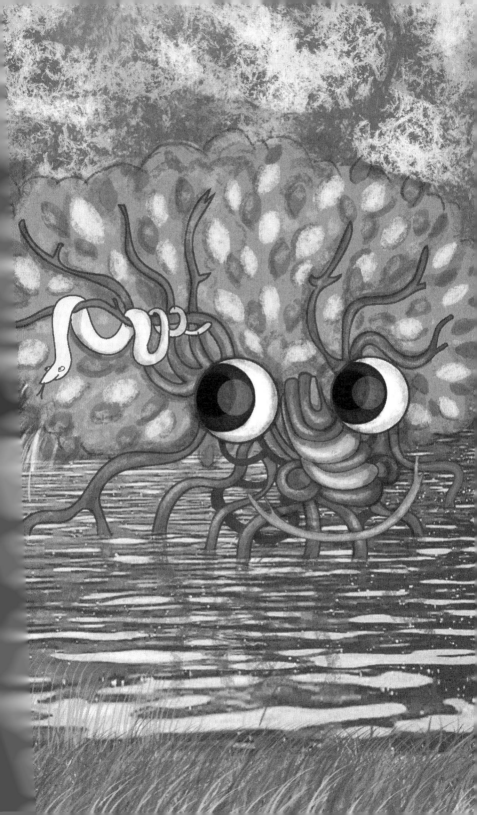

"Thank you, dear. That's what I always say'sss. But there is something else we do'sss," the mangrove hissed happily. "We absorb the power of the wind. Our roots break the waves'sss so Kukulkan has less power where we live'sss. That's why he hates us'sss."

"Then that's the solution! Let's plant more mangroves!" Ti shouted excitedly.

"No!" Nuuk Ha replied loudly.

Confused, Ti turned to the turtle. "Why not?"

"Because you have to go and find the next key before Kukulkan does. You must continue your journey. I will stay here and plant more mangroves."

"Please don't leave me," Ti begged.

"I know it's hard. But I wouldn't survive in the jungle. There are too many dangers for a turtle. The jungle is not my element. I wouldn't be of any help to you," the turtle responded softly.

"But I really want you to come," urged Ti.

"We will see each other again. Come on, let's enjoy the time we still have together," and Nuuk Ha dove into the water with a big smile on her face.

After a long bath, Nuuk Ha and Ti sat down under some palm trees, enjoying the shade. As they sipped fresh coconut water, Ti pondered his journey.

"How do I find the second key? And who might know where Sian Ka'an is?"

"Very good questions," the turtle acknowledged. "Hey mangrove, who knows where Sian Ka'an is?" she called out.

"Ask the manatee that sleeps over there in the shallow water'sss," the mangrove replied.

"Mana-what?" Ti wondered, looking over towards what looked like a lagoon.

When Nuuk Ha and the boy drew nearer to the water, they saw a strange looking animal with a big belly sleeping in the shallow lagoon. It had a dark rock-like color, a pair of front flippers and a horizontally flattened tail to swim.

"I am sorry to interrupt, but do you know where Sian Ka'an is?" Ti asked politely.

The manatee opened one eye and looked at the unlikely travelers. With a big yawn, it answered: "very funny. You are in Sian Ka'an, but I really suggest you have a nap. Best activity of the day."

Ti and Nuuk Ha looked puzzled. "*This* is Sian Ka'an?" they both exclaimed simultaneously.

"But where did your grandfather hide the key? I doubt he just threw it into the lagoon," the turtle said, confused.

"Is there a temple or a city in Sian Ka'an?" Ti consulted the manatee.

"I don't know, but I can ask my sister," said the manatee, who then released a high-pitched sound that was answered from further away instantly. "My sister says there is a town called Muyil. She said to follow the lagoon inland." And with that, the manatee went back to sleep.

"We found the boy in Sian Ka'an. He looks unhurt. What do you want me to do next?" the god of travelers, Xaman Ek, asked Itzamna.

"Do you know where Kukulkan is?" Itzamna replied.

"No. But I haven't spotted him anywhere near the boy."

"Good. Thank you. You can go. I will take care of it from here on," said Itzamna sending Xaman Ek away. When the sun started to set, Itzamna climbed the ninety-one steps of the pyramid. With a deep breath he took the final step onto the ceremonial platform at the top of the pyramid. The god gazed out over the beautiful jungle that surrounded the city of Chichen Itza. He sat down, positioning himself towards Sian Ka'an, and in deep concentration Itzamna sent a message to a priest he trusted with the life of Ti.

Lak'in, please find this boy and watch out for him. He should be near you. I sent him on the journey to secure our happiness, but he is in great danger. I ask that you give him shelter and protection.'

Long after, Itzamna sat in silence on top of the pyramid watching the day turn into night, the light making space for the darkness, and the moon replacing the sun. "Everything is in motion, always," observed the god.

The next morning, Ti set out on his journey with the directions to Muyil. He followed the lagoon inland as the manatee had told him. Before his departure, Nuuk Ha and he had discussed that Ti should look for a temple or a pyramid in the city. Determined to find the second key, Ti ignored the exhaustion that threatened to overcome him.

"Hi! Do you need a ride?" a young voice unexpectedly piped up. Ti turned around to see a girl and boy in a canoe packed with food and clothes.

"Yes, thank you! Where are you going?" Ti replied.

"Muyil," the girl answered.

"Come on, hop in!" said the boy and invited Ti into the canoe. Ti took a seat next to the girl. Shyly, he looked at his new travel companions.

"How long will it take to get to Muyil?" Ti asked.

"Long enough to sing all of our favorite songs," the girl said, laughing as she began to sing.

Nobody paid attention to the long-tailed bird sitting on a branch, watching them from above.

When they reached the shore of the lagoon, the young boy steered the canoe in between the other parked boats that sleepily bobbed to the rhythm of the lapping water. The boy effortlessly jumped out of the canoe and docked it at a wooden pole.

"Kiik, give me your hand," he invited his sister.

"Ti first," the girl answered. Ti stood up, trying to balance his weight so as not to fall into the lagoon. Kiik started moving the canoe from side to side so it was impossible for him to take another step. The girl doubled over with laughter.

"This isn't funny. Stop it!" Ti shouted, aggravated. But when he saw Kiik holding her belly from laughing, he had to chuckle too.

Tukuul watched his sister and Ti stonily. "Can we go now?" he asked, annoyed at their laughter.

Kiik crawled off the canoe on all fours, still laughing. "You should have seen your face," she said. "That was too funny."

Ti found the girl's laugh so contagious that he couldn't stop laughing too.

"When you're done, you can come to the house.

I'm leaving now to get help unloading the boat," Tukuul said, stomping off.

"I think your brother is mad," Ti said, finally getting a handle on his laughter.

"Don't worry about him. Come, let me show you Muyil," said Kiik over her shoulder to Ti as she began following a dirt path. Dense jungle surrounded them. Ti had to pay close attention so he wouldn't fall over the large roots that crossed the narrow road.

"We're almost there," said Kiik encouragingly and started running.

"Wait, I can't see you anymore!" he shouted. But just as Ti started feeling uneasy, he came upon a bustling market place. Everyone was moving around quickly, some shouting orders, others carrying goods. Ti saw golden honey, beautiful jewelry made out of jade, feathers, chewing gum, and salt being packed, weighed and re-packed again. Thirteen buildings were built to form a horseshoe shape on the raised plateau, overlooking the hectic activity of the town. Their decorative paintings in black and blue gleamed in sharp contrast to the lush green of the jungle. Fascinated, Ti looked around. His gaze landed upon Kiik amongst a group of people. She waved happily at Ti, gesturing for him to join her.

"You *have* to try the chocolate," she said, holding a pottery cup up to his face.

An irresistible smell rose up to Ti's nose. Cautiously, he took his first sip. It was the best drink he had ever had. It was so delicious that Ti didn't want to swallow it, so he stood amongst people he didn't know with his eyes and mouth closed, fully enjoying the sweet experience.

"Hey, are you still alive?" Kiik asked, giving him a slight nudge with her elbow.

Ti tried to smile, but chocolate started dripping from his mouth.

"You know you need to swallow it, right?" the girl asked, grinning.

Ti nodded, but couldn't stop snorting when he started imagining how he must look. Chocolate came shooting straight out of his nose. Ti started coughing so loud that everybody stopped in their tracks to see what had just happened. His face scarlet with embarrassment, Ti waved his arm to signal that he was all right.

An elderly woman came over and put her hand on his shoulder. "Are you ok, young one?" she asked. "Kiik, is he your friend?"

"Yes, Grandma. Tukuul and I met him at the lagoon. His name is Ti," Kiik answered politely.

"Bring him to our house. He must be hungry," Kiik's grandmother suggested.

Kiik and Ti passed many houses, all of similar shapes and sizes. Most of them were rectangular with mud walls and thatched roofs.

Ti looked around inquisitively. The houses weren't much different from his own that he left what felt like such a long time ago. He realized how much he missed his parents and friends. Suddenly Ti hated the journey his grandfather had put upon him and a burning desire to return home took over. His sadness gave way to anger, anger that he had been chosen for a journey he had never asked for; a journey that was dangerous and had separated him from his family. But it was also the journey that had led him here, next to the girl he had just met.

"What a lovely meal you prepared for me," Ixchel said.

Itzamna looked up from his plate. "You have been gone for so long that I wanted to surprise you. Now, tell me about your journey."

"I don't want to bore you with the details," the goddess answered evasively.

"You don't bore me. I love to hear what you have done and seen," Itzamna insisted and took another bite.

"Well, as you know, I went to my island Cozumel to check that everything was in order," Ixchel informed him dully.

"Were many women there?" her husband asked.

"Yes, and they all want the same thing. Babies, babies, babies. Is there really nothing else to ask for?" she replied, aggravated.

"Ixchel!" Itzamna exclaimed, outraged at what he just had heard. "You are the goddess of fertility. Women come to you for help. How can you say such a horrible thing?"

"I knew you wouldn't understand. You have so many powers. You can do so many things. And what do I have? Floods and fertility," Ixchel shouted angrily.

"And what a beautiful power to have. Creating *life*
Ixchel," Itzamna replied, taking his wife's hand.
"It's boring. I want to have more power. I want to
rule! You should tell me where the keys are hidden,"
she muttered under her breath.

"What did you just say?" Itzamna shouted, his voice echoing off the walls. "How do you know about the keys?"

Petrified, Ixchel stood rigid. She looked up, staring at her husband.

"You announced it at the meeting of the highest gods. Don't you remember? You told us you had decided to hide the keys. But let us finish our dinner you prepared and forget about it. We shouldn't fight on my first day back," Ixchel said, pulling Itzamna back to the table.

Quietly they finished their food, but a tiny nagging doubt in Itzamna's head kept saying, *"I don't remember talking about the keys that night."*

18

It was dark when the Quetzal was on his way back to Kukulkan. He flew quickly, eager to tell Kukulkan what he had seen. The deity was standing on top of the temple of Tulum, scanning the sky for his messenger. He breathed in the salty smell of the ocean, his arms wide open.

A small fire burned restlessly inside the temple, illuminating the night to help direct sea travelers. The fire logs crackled quietly and fitfully when the Quetzal finally landed on Kukulkan's arm.

"My feathered friend, it fills me with great pleasure that you have returned to me. Now, please tell me what you have seen," Kukulkan commanded the Quetzal.

An excited chirp was the answer to the god's question. "Is he by himself or does he have company on the way to Muyil?" Kukulkan asked the bird. A long deep chirp pierced the night.

"A brother and sister?! Well, it's easier for me to control someone's will who is unhappy, so who do you think I should use?"

The Quetzal looked thoughtfully in the sky before he answered the god with a chirp.

"Ok. It is decided then. I will possess the boy," determined Kukulkan, pulling a feather out of his hat. The bird took the feather in his beak. "Go fly back my friend and touch the boy's face with this feather," the deity ordered, and lifted his arm up quickly for the bird to take off.

Kukulkan remained on top of the temple watching the Quetzal getting smaller and smaller until the tiny red dot in the far distance disappeared and only the starless sky remained. He turned to the ocean and called to the winds. Stronger and stronger they came, stirring the waves higher and higher.

"I will be the most powerful of all when all keys are in my possession. I will direct every element, every human and every creature in this world. Terror and fear shall be my rule. There will be no laughter under my regime," Kukulkan howled into the night.

No one responded except the ocean, crashing its waves relentlessly against the walls of the city of Tulum.

19

That same night, Itzamna wandered into the jungle. The human world was asleep but the jungle vibrated with life. There was a rustle to the left, a crackle to the right and the howling call of a monkey higher up. The fresh air felt good and Itzamna inhaled it deeply. Once he reached the sacred tree, he made himself comfortable on the ground.

"It has been too long since I last visited you," Itzamna greeted the Ceiba tree, the symbol of the universe. He leaned against its strong trunk, stretched out his legs and looked up to marvel at the tree's high branches with its thorns and ivory flowers. It was that beautiful time of year when the tree was blossoming. Admiring the beauty that surrounded him, the voices in his head began to calm, and once his emotions settled, the deity slowly wandered into the far reaches of his memory.

Itzamna concentrated deeply in order not to miss any detail from what he sought from the past.

There he was, many moons ago, back in the temple with the gods sitting in front of him. It was the night he had to announce the return of Kukulkan. Only a few torches were lit, slowly burning on the walls.

He saw Ixchel with the snake on her head sitting in the front row. Next to her on the right was Ixcacao, nibbling nervously on her chocolate. The tension amongst the gods was tangible and fear filled the air after Itzamna had announced his apprehension. "... I have decided that it would be best to hide THE KEY," the god heard himself saying so long ago.

Itzamna moved the scene forward to the end of the meeting and saw himself punching smaller keys out of the original one, out of sight of the other gods. Shortly after, the great Shaman Tat had entered the room to receive the small keys. "Leave Chichen Itza and hide each key in a different location so that under no circumstances can Kukulkan find them," Itzamna again heard himself instructing Tat.

The god went back and forth amongst the scenes of his memories, observing every detail. Over and over again he played back the speech he had given, but it became clear that he had never mentioned the small keys to Ixchel or any of the other gods.

He was stunned. "She lied to me. I have put the boy in grave danger," he admitted to himself angrily.

Everybody was asleep. Ti had waited patiently to hear the rhythmic breathing of Kiik and her family to make sure nobody would notice what he was about to do. Slowly he got up and tiptoed out of the house.

Ti knew exactly where he was headed. During the day, when Kiik had shown him around, he had spotted a building that looked like a perfect hiding place for the second key.

Making sure he had no uninvited observers, Ti carefully looked around while crossing the plateau. Things looked different at night, but he could easily make out the highest building in Muyil. The upper temple at its top had a solid, circular tower with three entrances to the west. Ti took a seat in front of the building facing the entrances and started playing the tune his grandfather had taught him on his golden shell. He closed his eyes as he had done in Tulum, where a before unseen path had opened up during his song, leading to the first key.

After he had finished the song, Ti opened his eyes to inspect the building.

He looked up to the temple but the three entrances seemed unchanged.

"Maybe I didn't concentrate enough," Ti said to himself and began to play the same tune again. But the result was equally disappointing.

Carefully he climbed the stairs to the upper temple. The room was tiny and cramped and made it difficult for him to move around. With both hands he felt every stone on the inside trying to find the second key. But the temple was not hiding what he was looking for.

Panic gripped him. Maybe this was not the right place. The inscription in Tulum had not said Muyil, after all. It had mentioned Sian Ka'an and Kiik had told him that it was a gigantic natural habitat. "I will never find the second key," Ti whispered, holding back tears.

He stood quietly, watching dark clouds approaching the city. Suddenly, the roar of thunder broke the silence in the far distance and interrupted the boy's thoughts.

Determination washed over him. "Of course I can find the second key. After all, it was my grandfather who hid it," Ti said out loud, punching his fist against the wall. "I will try again tomorrow." He ran quickly back to the house before the rain began to fall.

It was not only Ti who was awake. Someone else had waited a long time for everyone to be asleep.

The tiny Quetzal had watched the house and fluttered into the open door after Ti had left. Peeking inside, the bird made out the girl and next to her the one he was looking for.

The Quetzal hopped silently inside the house next to Tukuul's head. He slowly pulled the feather Kukulkan had given him in Tulum out of his plumage and gently touched the boy's face. A clap of thunder confirmed that Kukulkan was close and had taken possession of Tukuul's will. Satisfied, the bird left the house, but did not depart the city of Muyil.

Only the stars above witnessed Itzamna reach into his bag and pull out a package which he slowly unfolded. Carefully, the god placed the fish on the ground and respectfully stepped away, awaiting the most sacred animal of all.

It wasn't long before a loud growl cut through the silence of the night. First a tan paw with black spots appeared, then a beautiful big cat emerged from between the trees and gracefully walked towards the deity.

"I thank you for coming, Balam," Itzamna welcomed the jaguar. "Please accept my gift," and he pointed towards the food.

The big cat smelled the fish and sat down to eat. Only when the jaguar had finished eating did the god approach him. "I need you to go to Sian Ka'an and find the priest Lak'in. He will guide you to the boy who I want you to accompany. You are the most powerful protector I can think of," Itzamna implored.

The jaguar's yellow eyes fixed on the old man in front of him. The world seemed to stand still until a smile crossed the cat's face. In a flash, the jaguar sprinted towards the jungle, balancing its weight with its long dark spotted tail.

"I hope he gets there in time," Itzamna whispered to himself anxiously, watching the jaguar disappear.

23

Deep in thought, Kukulkan walked the deserted grounds of Tulum, his hands folded behind his back. Ixchel appeared through one of the entrances of the protecting walls. "I'm back," the goddess announced. "Good," the deity irritably replied. "What have you found out?"

Ixchel looked startled when she saw Kukulkan up close. The god's face looked emaciated and pale. "When was the last time you slept?" she asked Kukulkan, alarmed.

"I have possessed the will of the brother, so my powers are split," Kukulkan explained. "Now, tell me the news," he demanded impatiently.

"You won't like what I have to tell you," Ixchel answered anxiously.

Kukulkan turned around and looked at her with fiery eyes. "What is it?"

"I said something to Itzamna that might have given him the idea that I am helping you find the keys," she guiltily confessed.

Kukulkan stood stock still, taking in what he had just heard. Only a tiny tick in his left eye gave away his tension.

"It's probably nothing and I'm just being overly concerned," Ixchel added quickly, attempting to diffuse the situation.

"You did what?!" he finally screamed.

"I'm sorry. Please forgive me," the goddess begged.

"No, I won't. You know I have to punish you for not being worthy of my trust," Kukulkan roared.

"Yes, I know," she said, falling on her knees to await her sentencing.

"This time as a warning I will take away your strongest power. You will remain the goddess of fertility only until you prove to me that I can trust you again. Now go get the sacred jar that enables you to command the floods and give it to me," Kukulkan ordered.

Ixchel slowly stood up to do as she had been told. "As you wish," she said softly.

Early in the morning, the tiny canoe docked in the lagoon of Muyil. Thousands of birds sang happily and glided above the beautiful water that mirrored their reflections in the rising sun.

An elderly man dressed in white got off the boat and with a serious look strode briskly towards the town. Heavy golden ornaments covered his wrists and ankles, identifying him as a high priest.

Lak'in was exhausted from his trip, especially because he hadn't found the boy. He had traveled the lagoons and canals all the way to the ocean but hadn't seen any sign of him. '*Maybe Itzamna was wrong and the boy is not in Sian Ka'an, or something happened to him,*' the priest worried to himself. '*I need to speak with Itzamna,*' he decided, and the high priest hastened his steps.

Kiik was preparing breakfast when her grandfather entered the house. "Good morning, Grandpa! How was your trip? Do you want some food?" she asked, throwing her arms around him.

Lak'in had to laugh, seeing the excitement of his granddaughter. "Yes, food would be wonderful. But let me first clean up," he said, and walked out of the kitchen when he bumped into Ti.

"Who's this?" the priest asked, surprised, looking between the two.

"This is Ti. He is really nice," Kiik explained, approaching her grandfather.

"But how did he get here?" Lak'in demanded. Just then he saw the golden shell around the boy's neck.

"Good morning. Kiik was nice enough to help me get to Muyil," Ti said, holding out his hand to greet the man in front of him.

The priest couldn't help but stare at the shell. Memories of a long-forgotten time flashed through his mind. 'Could this really be?' he wondered.

"Grandpa!" Kiik exclaimed, interrupting Lak'in's thoughts.

"Yes, yes. Hello. Nice to meet you," stuttered the priest and shook Ti's hand. "Can you play that shell?" Lak'in asked, pointing at the boy's neck.

"Yes I can. Would you like to hear a song?" Ti politely offered.

"Please." Lak'in nervously leaned back against the wall.

"I will play you my favorite song, one that someone very special taught me," said Ti, and started the tune his grandfather had shown him only to be interrupted by the old man storming out of the house after the first few notes.

"He's usually a lot more normal," Kiik said to Ti apologetically.

26

"It's him. I can't believe it. He's here to get the key," Lak'in muttered, rushing to the blacksmith.

Swiftly he took off one of his golden bracelets and put it in the oven to melt. The priest watched the fire liquefy the beautiful metal. There, in between the flames, a tiny key began to materialize.

Hypnotized by the fire, Lak'in started talking to his deceased friend. "Tat, I am doubtful. The boy who is coming for the key is the same boy Itzamna asked me to protect. I promised you a long time ago to hand over the key to whomever could play that song on a golden shell, but I am truly worried. I hope there are things I do not know yet."

The moment couldn't have been more perfect for a long spotted tail to twine around the priest's legs. A soft growl made Lak'in look down. A jaguar sat in front of him, licking its fur. He did not seem to be in a rush and thoroughly cleaned every paw before he finally directed his words at the priest. "I am here to protect the boy. So do what you are destined to do," and the jaguar walked away with a swagger, leaving Lak'in behind.

When the fire finally extinguished itself, the priest took the key out of the oven. He put it in his pocket, until the shelter of darkness would allow him to give it to Ti.

27

"Ti! Wake up!" a voice whispered close to the boy's ear. A hand shook him lightly. "You have to come with me."

Ti took a few moments to recognize Lak'in standing next to him.

Without asking any questions, he got up and followed Kiik's grandfather out of the house. Silently they walked next to each other with the unspoken understanding that what was about to happen next was important.

"Stay here. I will be back shortly," Lak'in said when they arrived at the building where Ti had assumed the key would be hidden.

He looked around and wondered if his grandfather Tat had ever stood in the same place.

When Lak'in came back, he was joined by a big cat.

"This is Balam," the priest introduced the jaguar. "He will accompany you on your journey." The old man pulled the key from his rope. "I have been hiding this key for many years, but now it's time for it to be revealed again." Slowly Lak'in took Ti's hand and placed the key into his palm.

"For you to fulfill your destiny, Chosen One, go to the place 'Where the Waters are Stirred by the Wind'. Trust that the power lies within you," the priest said in a powerful voice.

Ti nodded and stored the second key in the golden shell next to the first one.

"Now go. Time is of the essence. It has been an honor to meet you," and Lak'in hugged Ti tightly. "Take care of yourself," and the old man walked away.

"Follow me," the jaguar said to Ti. The cat paused for a quick moment. "Hmmm. I thought I heard something. We should hurry," and together they left Muyil.

28

The house was dark and quiet when Kukulkan, through the eyes of Tukuul, saw the shadow come closer, whispering something into Ti's ear.

The old man who seemed to be a priest of some sort helped the boy get up and together they left the house, careful to make no noise.

Kukulkan, disguised as Tukuul, followed Ti and the priest to the center of Muyil and when they reached their destination, the old man gave instructions to Ti and disappeared into the darkness.

The god slid between the buildings, trying to get closer to hear what they were saying. 'Where is the old man? What is he doing?' Kukulkan wondered.

A big cat appeared and confidently sauntered along beside the priest.

"What is that supposed to mean? Where did that jaguar come from? I have to be extra careful," the deity whispered. Kukulkan chewed Tukuul's lip, nervously watching the three in front of him. He knew the moment was close and Tukuul's entire body tensed with excitement.

Finally, the priest pulled the key out of his dress and gave it to Ti.

"Speak up old man! I can't hear you!" Kukulkan hissed angrily, but they were too far away and he couldn't risk getting any closer. *'So the old man stays here, and Ti and the jaguar are leaving. Perfect. I will follow them and steal the keys. But I need to find a way to get rid of that cat.'* The deity masqueraded as Tukuul strode forward and accidentally stepped on a tiny branch that broke under his weight. Kukulkan saw the jaguar pause, so he pressed Tukuul's back against the wall and held his breath until he saw the jaguar and Ti finally leave Muyil. Snake-like, he peeled himself off the building to follow what he desired the most.

Tulum

Muyil

×

Sian Ka'an

Kiik woke up early. She stretched her arms above her head, yawned loudly and jumped out of her hammock. She loved mornings.

The house was dark and quiet. But the morning light already occupied a small portion of the entrance and a few rays of sun had found their way into the inside through gaps in the wall.

The girl didn't want to wake anybody and bent down to walk below the hammocks, but accidentally jostled the one Ti was sleeping in. Without resistance the thick tissue moved to the side. Kiik stopped and wondered. The hammock could not move that easily with someone inside unless Ti wasn't in it! But where could he be at this time of the day?!

Kiik looked and saw that the hammock was indeed empty. She headed towards the entrance but when she passed her brother's hammock, she saw that he wasn't in it either. 'What's going on?' she wondered, worried. Her brother never got up until she turned his hammock upside down so he would almost fall out of it.

Kiik stuck her head outside the house and looked around but didn't see anybody.

"Grandfather, wake up!" she said and shook the old man in his hammock.

"What is it Kiik?" growled Lak'in sleepily.

"Ti and Tukuul are not in the house. I can't find them!" she explained urgently.

Slowly the priest sat up and looked at his granddaughter. "Listen, Kiik. Ti had to leave Muyil. There is something he needs to do."

"What? When? Why didn't he say goodbye?" Kiik asked, starting to get upset.

"There was no time for goodbyes. He didn't know himself that he was leaving so quickly," Lak'in calmly replied.

"And Tukuul? Where is he? Did he have anything important to do as well in the middle of the night?" the girl asked furiously and ran outside trying to walk off her anger. She felt left out.

Kiik wandered aimlessly around until something on the wall of one of the buildings around the highest temple caught her attention. She got closer to have a better look. The strange thing seemed to be a snake skin but the piece on the wall was far too big to be a regular snake. It was almost the size of a human being. Kiik peeled the skin off the wall and ran with it to the house.

"Look, what I found grandfather!"

Lak'in looked at the snake skin and with panic in his voice asked, "Where did you find this?"

"Close to the highest temple. It was on one of the walls."

Quickly the priest started packing a few things. "Oh no, oh no. This cannot be good", he muttered under his breath. "I have to leave. Kiss your grandmother for me when she gets up," Lak'in said to Kiik as he rushed around.

"I want to come with you!" the girl said.

"No, it is too dangerous," her grandfather replied.

"I will come with you," Kiik repeated in a tone that didn't leave room for argument. "I am the best tracker there is."

Lak'in deliberated for a minute and finally decided. "Ok. But we have to leave now."

Shortly after, they departed Muyil with mixed emotions; Lak'in concerned about who had seen him and Ti the night before, and Kiik excited for an adventure.

TI´S WEBSITE
with more infos on the Mayan calendar, mangroves, sinkholes...

www.tiandthemagicalkey.com

MAYAN CALENDAR

SINKHOLES

MANGROVES

BUY BOOK

SEND US A PICTURE OF YOUR CHILD WITH THE BOOK and WE POST IT ON

www.tiandthemagicalkey.com

Email:
team@tiandthemagicalkey.com

www.facebook.com/tiandthe magicalkey

TI'S FIRST ADVENTURE
TI AND THE MAGICAL KEY™
HOW IT ALL BEGAN

Available on Amazon and
http://www.tiandthemagicalkey.com/buy-book.html

COME VISIT TI'S SHOP – many more products at
http://www.tiandthemagicalkey.com/shop.html

Made in the USA
Charleston, SC
01 March 2016